I0618029

For my goddaughter Laila

- Nahjee

For brave, beautiful Francisca

- Emily

Text copyright © Nahjee Grant 2017
Illustrations copyright © Emily Stewart 2017
Printed in the United States of America

For more information please visit:
www.nahjeegrant.com
www.emilydstewart.com

Where Did My Dream Go?

Written by Nahjee Grant

Illustrated by Emily D. Stewart

ALL CHILDREN EQUAL SUCCESS

One morning, Jasmine woke up to the smell of breakfast and the melody of birds singing near her window. Usually, she woke to memories of her dreams from the night before. On that particular morning, however, she couldn't remember a thing. She sat up on the bed, worried and wondering: *Where did my dream go? I see my dreams every night, yet this one has disappeared!*

Most days she could remember her dreams vividly. When she was 6, she dreamt she was an astronaut— skipping from planet to planet, flying among the brightest stars. One year later, she was a firefighter saving children from a burning building. Five days after that, she dreamt she was a police officer fighting crime in the neighborhood. On her 8th birthday, she was a soccer star who scored the winning goal. She had always remembered those dreams. But this one was different.

Getting ready for school, she swept memories of her earlier dreams under the bed for safe keeping, and tried to remember the dream that she lost from the night before.

She was on a mission. *Where is my dream? I will not stop until I find it.*

Still struggling to find where her dream had disappeared to, she made her way downstairs. Her mom walked out from the kitchen with a bowl of cereal and juice, but Jasmine had lost her appetite.

"I can't remember my dream," said Jasmine. "What am I going to do?"

"You are a fearless child who never gives up until you find what you are looking for," her mother replied. "There are signs everywhere that will help you find it. I'm sure it's hiding for a reason and will show up at the right time, so be ready when it does. Now finish breakfast and get ready for the bus."

Jasmine was still worried. She didn't talk to anyone on the bus because she was busy searching for clues on her way to school.

At school, she searched her cubby: I have to find my dream. *What if it doesn't turn up? What if my dream is lost forever? I may never go back to sleep again!*

The bell rang. Jasmine made her way to class, feeling determined. She heard her mom's voice in her head: *You are fearless and never give up.*

During math, Mr. Smith asked the class for an answer to a question. Jasmine, who usually hated to talk in class, confidently raised her hand. "I have the answer. I think 5 x 70=350."

"Well, yes it is. Great job, Jasmine," he replied. "You see class, if you believe you know the answer, don't be afraid to give it a try. And if you don't know, it's okay to ask for help."

After class, Jasmine asked her friends what they had dreamed about the night before. She hoped their answers would remind her of her own dream. Micah said even though he has trouble reading, he always dreams of being an author. Ayana, the quietest kid in class, was a famous actress in her dreams.

"Wow those dreams are amazing!" Jasmine replied, feeling sad that she still could not remember hers.

At recess, Jasmine noticed a new swing set on the playground. Humming a tune, she nervously rolled onto the access platform, feeling a little shaky as she tried it out for her first time. As she began to swing higher and higher, she wondered whether it was worth continuing her search. She had always been told "the sky's the limit." But her dream from the night before seemed just beyond her reach.

After recess, Jasmine's class took a trip to the one place that always gave her peace, the library. *Books are full of information and knowledge,* she said to herself. *Maybe I'll find a book that will explain what happens to dreams that disappear and how to recover a dream you lose.*

Jasmine was just finishing reading a wonderful story when a voice on the loudspeaker interrupted her thoughts: "Excuse me everyone, the school talent show will take place at 1 pm. Students, please make your way to the auditorium. All presenters should report backstage immediately."

In a panic, Jasmine dropped her book and headed toward the exit.

"Oh no!" she said, "I searched for my dream for so long that I forgot I signed up for the talent show. This has to be the worst day of my life! I'm not prepared or focused, and right now I do not want to perform in front of anyone." She struggled to hold back tears as she zipped down the hall on her way backstage.

As she waited with the other performers, she pulled the curtain back to check the size of the crowd.

"Wow that's a lot of people watching. I don't think I have what it takes. I didn't practice enough. Maybe if I sneak out, no one will notice," she said. Jasmine was heading toward the exit when she suddenly heard her name called next.

Her heart was pounding and her palms were sweaty, making it difficult to control her chair as she rolled onto the stage.

She gripped the microphone, thinking, *Why did I ever decide to chase a silly dream I cannot remember? I will never get distracted by following my dreams again!*

As she squeezed the microphone tightly in her hands and fear began to take over, she suddenly remembered: her dream was to motivate millions of kids with inspiring songs. It was never really lost; and this was the moment to show everyone just how confident she really was!

Jasmine took a deep breath, and confidently sang her favorite song, the one about daring to follow your dreams and not being afraid to be who you are.

As she sang the last note, there was a thunderous applause. She opened her eyes to see her classmates jumping up and down, cheering her on. Her teachers had tears of joy in their eyes.

When Jasmine went to bed that night, she realized her dream had never truly disappeared. It had been hiding inside her all along. Dreams don't always return. But this one was worth looking for. So remember to always follow your dreams.